# THE KIDS'
# EARTH
# HANDBOOK

## Books by
## SANDRA MARKLE

Exploring Winter
Exploring Summer
Exploring Spring
Exploring Autumn
Science Mini-Mysteries
Power Up
The Kids' Earth Handbook

# THE KIDS' EARTH HANDBOOK

## Sandra Markle

## Atheneum 1991 New York

**Maxwell Macmillan Canada**   Toronto

**Maxwell Macmillan International**
New York   Oxford   Singapore   Sydney

*For Marcia Marshall who shares my appreciation for our special planet and whose editorial advice has always been very down to earth*

*The author would especially like to acknowledge the expertise and assistance provided by Dr. David A. Zuberer of Texas A&M University; Martha Swiss, Air & Waste Management; and Dr. Robert Roe, Jr., winner of the James Bryant Connant national award in chemistry.*

| Photo Credits | Page |
| --- | --- |
| Steve Foxall, Dallas, Texas | 2, 19 |
| National Aeronautics and Space Administration | 3 |
| Dr. David A. Zuberer, Texas A&M University | 7, 9 |
| New York City Department of Sanitation, Bureau of Public Affairs | 24 |
| The Garbage Project, University of Arizona | 26 |
| Agripost, Inc. | 28–29 |
| National Park Service | 42 |

*This book is printed on recycled paper.*

Library of Congress Cataloging-in-Publication Data
Markle, Sandra. The kids' earth handbook/by Sandra Markle.—1st ed. p.     cm. Summary: Presents activities and experiments which demonstrate how living things interact with each other and the environment. Includes instructions for making miniature ecosystems. ISBN 0–689–31707–7  1. Environmental protection—Citizen participation—Juvenile literature. 2. Pollution—Experiments—Juvenile literature. 3. Environmental protection—Experiments—Juvenile literature. [1. Environmental protection—Experiments. 2. Pollution—Experiments. 3. Experiments.] I. Title. TD171.7.M37     1991 363.7—dc20 90–27478

# Contents

The Journey Begins        1

Can You Get Clean Water from Dirty Water?        4

The Great Balancing Trick        6

Where Did the Energy Go?        8

Two Mysteries        10

Biosphere II: Earth's Sequel        11

Why Do We Need Forests?        13

What Would You Do?        14

Adopt a Tree        15

Trees Are Air Conditioners        18

Rain Forests Are Special        19

After the Forest Is Gone        21

Fast Fact        22

Study Wildlife at the Zoo        22

A Brief History of Trash        23

Digging into Landfills        25

Make Natural Fertilizer from Garbage        27

Can You Use Less More Often?        29

Does Your Home Have Hazardous Wastes?        30

Just as Good the Second Time Around        31

What's in the Trash?        32

Be a Recycling Inventor        33

Paper Facts        34

What about Plastics?        35

Longer Summers Could Cause Hot Problems        36

How Much Excess $CO_2$ Do You Add?        40

More Sunscreen Needed        41

Acid Rain Keeps Falling on My Head      43
Acid Rain in Your Miniworld      44
Check for Dirty Air      45
Making Air Healthier      46
Rivers in Danger      49
Adopt a Stream or River      50
Water: Good to the Last Drop      51
Cleaning Water to Be Used Again      53
Oil and Water Don't Mix      55
No Slick Solution      56
The Journey Continues      57
Index      58

# The Journey Begins

What if you were about to board a spaceship for a trip across the galaxy that would last many years? Your spaceship would have to supply you with everything you needed to survive: air with just the right amount of oxygen, drinkable water, food, shelter from anything that might harm you, and warmth. You'd need some way to get rid of your body's wastes and any trash or garbage that piled up. It would also be a much more pleasant and interesting trip if you didn't have to go alone.

Well, guess what? You are on a spaceship called Earth. It's a lot bigger than any space shuttle or space station that has been launched so far, but its life support systems are basically the same. So are its challenges: managing life support systems so they function properly; dealing with problems such as pollutants; having only a limited supply of resources; and sharing everything on board with all the other members of your expedition's team.

To develop an appreciation for how living things interact with one another and the environment on a space station or planet, you can build a miniworld—a terrarium. First, you'll need a container such as a glass aquarium or a gallon-sized clear glass or plastic jar with a large mouth. Then you'll need to think about

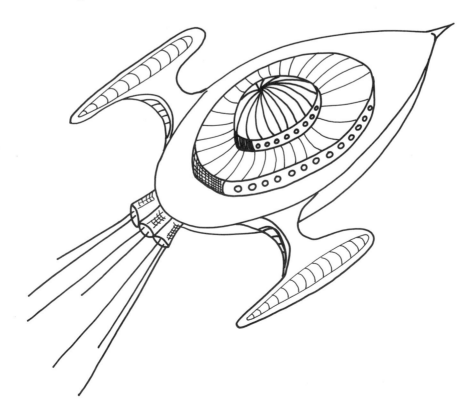

the key elements: land, water, and air. Your miniworld could be a desert; a tropical rain forest or a deciduous forest where trees lose their leaves during part of the year; a coniferous forest; a grassland; a tundra (a very cold environment); a freshwater pond; an estuary (a region where fresh water and salt water mix); or a small ocean. The conditions for some of these different environments are much more difficult to set up than for others. But with the right equipment, you could do it.

To keep this terrarium project inexpensive and easy, create a miniature grassland. Wash, rinse, and dry your container so it is clean, and cover the bottom with gravel or pebbles. Next, look for small plants growing close to your home that you can dig up and put in your terrarium. Be sure to dig up as much of the plants' roots as possible and collect soil from around these plants. Spread this soil over the gravel in your terrarium about two or three inches deep. If you don't have access to any outdoor plants, use potting soil and small houseplants like ferns and spider plants.

Before you plant, decide where the plants will go, making sure you've allowed enough room for growth. Then dig a hole for each plant, gently push the roots into the hole, and cover them with soil. Add rocks and pieces of wood to create a natural scene. Sprinkle the soil with just enough water to dampen it and spread

grass seed over any remaining patches of bare earth. Finally, put on the lid, or cover with clear plastic wrap.

Over the next few days, frequently check on the terrarium and record your observations in a notebook. Do the plants look healthy? Notice that drops of water collect and drip from the plastic cover or "rain" down the sides of the container.

How long your terrarium can support healthy life will depend on the success of these key cycles: the water cycle, the oxygen–carbon dioxide gas cycle, and the nutrient cycle. Just as your birthday and favorite holidays arrive the same time each year, these cycles can be counted on to repeat over and over. In the activities ahead, you'll investigate how these life-supporting cycles work—naturally, on earth, and with the help of special technology in man-made "mini-worlds." You'll also explore problems that threaten the earth, and you'll discover what's being done to solve these problems, what still needs work, and what you can do to help. This handbook is action-packed with lots of investigations and experiments. There are also challenges to start you thinking, facts that will amaze you, and the names and addresses of organizations you can write to for more information.

Your voyage aboard the Spaceship Earth has already started: It began the day you were born. And how successfully the earth's vital life-supporting systems function already depend, in part, on you. So don't wait to start learning more about how to maintain and even improve the earth. And hang on to the terrarium you built. You'll need it to perform some of the investigations you'll encounter later.

From space, it's easy to see that the life-supporting atmosphere, or layers of air, is only a thin envelope surrounding the earth.

# Can You Get Clean Water from Dirty Water?

Perform this investigation to find out. You'll need a two-liter clear-plastic soft-drink bottle, scissors, a glass, red food coloring, a teaspoonful of soil, clear plastic wrap, warm water, masking tape, a sturdy paper bowl, and ice cubes.

Cut off the neck of the bottle, making the edges as smooth as possible. Pour enough warm water into the bottle to fill it about two inches deep. Add enough food coloring to make the water bright red, and stir in the soil. Set the glass in the center of the dirty water. Cover the top of the bottle with plastic wrap and make the plastic dip down slightly over the glass as shown. Anchor the wrap in place with tape, sealing the edges. Set the paper bowl on top of the plastic and put five or six ice cubes in it.

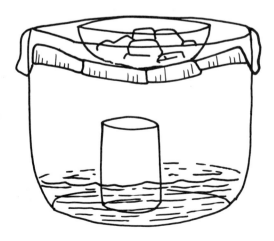

After an hour, remove the cover and carefully lift out the glass. There should now be a small amount of water in it. Look closely and you'll discover that this water is clear—not red or dirty. But just to be completely safe, don't drink it. This water really should be clean enough to drink; it is recycled water.

The sun heats water in ponds, lakes, and even the ocean. Water, like everything on earth, is made up of molecules, tiny building blocks of matter. As the water near the surface heats up, the molecules move faster and faster, bumping into one another and bouncing apart. And as this happens, the warmed liquid water evaporates, or changes to a gas called water vapor, and rises into the air. Particles of dirt, salt in the ocean, and even food coloring are heavier than the water molecules, so when water evaporates, any particles suspended in the water remain behind.

High in the atmosphere, the water molecules cool off, slow down, and begin to cling together forming tiny droplets of water. These form clouds in the sky. Eventually, if enough droplets combine, they become big drops too heavy to stay suspended in the air, and they fall as rain. Some of the water that lands on the earth soaks in, but most of it runs off, returning to ponds, lakes, and the oceans.

The water you collected in the cup was cleansed as it passed through the water cycle inside your closed system. Now take a close look at your mini-world, looking for evidence of the water cycle in action. How does this cycle help the plants?

WATER CYCLE

# The Great Balancing Trick

Dr. Clair Folsome, working at the University of Hawaii, built some completely sealed miniworlds that continued to be self-sustaining for more than ten years. These glass spheres, called ecospheres, contained shrimp (animals) and algae (green plants) in an ocean environment. It was a good beginning in the effort to understand what was needed for such a closed system to support life. For one thing, the amount of oxygen and carbon dioxide present in the system had to be carefully balanced to fit the needs of the animals and plants. An ecosystem is an area in nature in which all the plants and animals living there interact with one another and the environment.

Green plants are the producers in an ecosystem. In a process called photosynthesis, green plants use the energy from sunlight, plus water and carbon dioxide, to produce food in the form of sugar. During this process, oxygen is given off as a waste gas. Animals are the consumers. Unable to make food within its own body, an animal uses oxygen in the process of changing the food it eats into the energy it needs to be active and to grow. In the following activity, you'll be able to see that the animals and plants within an ecosystem are dependent on each other.

You'll need four clear plastic cups, water, two two-inch-long pieces of the water plant elodea, two small water snails nearly identical in size, a test kit for testing the pH level of the water, clear plastic wrap, a straw, and four rubber bands big enough to fit around the plastic cup. (Elodea, water snails, and pH test kits are available at stores that carry aquarium supplies.)

First fill all four cups with water and let them sit overnight. In the morning, add three drops of the blue indicator solution in the test kit to each of the four cups and set one of them aside. Place a snail in one of the remaining cups; a piece of elodea in another cup; and both a snail and a piece of elodea in the last cup. Seal the tops of all four cups tightly with clear wrap, anchoring the covers with rubber bands, and place the cups side by side in a brightly lit spot—but not in direct sunlight. When it gets dark that evening, check the results.

The test-kit solution that turned the water blue is an indicator, which means that it is something that changes color to show when a certain chemical is present. In this case, the indicator makes the blue water appear green to yellow when there is an acid present. You are probably fa-

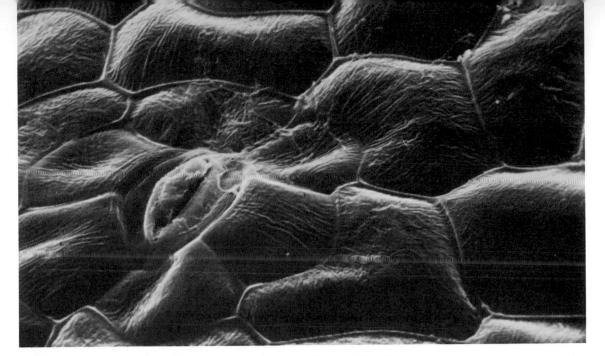

In this photo of the surface of a leaf magnified 2,500 times, you can clearly see the individual plant cells and one of the many cell openings, called stomata. Stomata allow carbon dioxide to enter the leaf and let oxygen out.

miliar with weak acids. Foods that taste sour, such as lemons and vinegar, contain weak acids. Oxygen and carbon dioxide are invisible as gases dissolved in water. Carbon dioxide, however, combines with water to form a weak acid. So if any carbon dioxide is present in the test water, the indicator's color change will let you know it's there.

In this test, you should discover that the cup containing the snail alone is the only one that has changed to green or yellow. This shows that the animal gives off carbon dioxide. The cups without any life forms, with only the plant, and with the snail and elodea together remain blue, showing that either no carbon dioxide is present or that the amount of oxygen balances the amount of carbon dioxide. (Note that if the amount of these two gases isn't quite balanced the color may change slightly, but not as much as with the snail alone.)

If you were to leave the cups sealed, eventually the snail alone and the elodea alone would die. The snail would use up all its available oxygen and the elodea would use up all its available carbon dioxide. The snail and elodea together, though, should survive—at least until the snail has eaten all the elodea—because each is supplying the other with the essential life-sustaining gas it needs. But don't wait to see these results. Take the snails and plants out of the test solutions and place them in a fishbowl or aquarium. Add freshwater fish, such as goldfish, to make an aquatic ecosystem you can continue to observe.

# Where Did the Energy Go?

You've already discovered that green plants are producers and that animals are consumers in an ecosystem. Some animals, such as mice, are plant eaters (herbivores) and get their energy in the form of sugars and starches produced and stored by plants. During this energy transfer, some of the energy is lost to the environment in the form of heat. The animal also uses up some for its own life activities—defending itself, finding a mate, and taking care of its young. Only a small amount of the energy gained from the plants is actually stored in the animal's body. This stored energy is what meat eaters (carnivores), such as snakes, receive when they eat a plant eater. And once again some of the energy flows away as heat during the transfer so this consumer must eat a number of plant eaters to get enough energy to support its life activities. The passage of energy from one level to another is called a food chain. The diminishing availability of energy creates a kind of pyramid of life within an ecosystem, with lots of green plants as the base, a large number of plant eaters at the second level, a smaller number of meat eaters at the third level, and only a tiny number of meat eaters at the top level receiving enough energy to survive.

Now imagine what would happen to the food chain illustrated by the life pyramid if all of one level, such as the snakes, was wiped out. If you predicted that the hawks would die, you'd be right—if the hawks only ate snakes. That's why many of the top-level consumers don't limit their diet to only one food item. Hawks, for example, also eat rabbits and mice, among other things. Some animal members of an ecosystem are omnivores and eat both plants and animals so they're sure to have a supply of food.

Besides producers and consumers there is one other group that plays an important role in the transfer of energy within an ecosystem—the decomposers. Take a look at the series of pictures that shows a pumpkin decomposing. The microscopic view lets you see a cluster of round bacterium called *micrococcus*. These tiny living organisms are attached to one of the thread-like filaments of the fungus you see growing on the pumpkin. The bacteria work with the fungus to decompose the pumpkin. Then when the pumpkin is completely decomposed, the fungus dies and the bacteria attacks it.

The decomposition is actually the result of many microorganisms digesting their food. During their digestion process, the single-celled microbes give off digestive juices that act on the surrounding material, breaking it down into a soluble form. Then the microbes absorb the nutrients they need to grow and

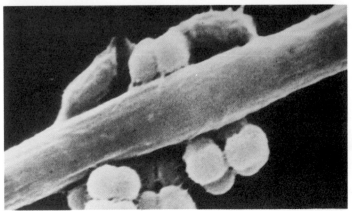

reproduce. They don't stop their digestion process when their needs are satisfied, though, and any excess nutrients remain in the soil or in the water if this process takes place in a pond or lake, or in the ocean. So minerals, such as phosphorous and nitrogen, which are essential to the growth of green plants, are made available to them. The plants absorb these minerals through their roots and use them during the process of photosynthesis to produce chemical energy in the form of sugar. And so the nutrient cycle begins all over again.

# Two Mysteries

Here are two true mysteries. To solve them, think about the earth's life-support systems and how they function. Then read the mysteries again and look for clues—anything that could disturb the normal balance between life and the environment. Decide what you think caused each of these mysterious events to occur before you read on.

**Mystery 1:** After Arizona's Kaibab Forest became a game reserve in 1906, government officials authorized the killing of mountain lions, coyotes, and wolves to protect the deer population. Over the next twenty years, hundreds of these predators were killed and the deer population rose from 4,000 to nearly 100,000. Then the number of deer began to drop drastically. By 1939, despite being protected, there fewer less than 10,000 deer left. Most of the predators were gone, so what killed all the deer?

**Mystery 2:** A heavy windstorm unexpectedly blew down whole groups of trees in Colorado's White River National Forest. Up until that time, the forest had been thriving. A few years after the storm, though, most of the forest was dead and the remaining trees were dying. What caused this forest to die?

Did you figure out what caused these mysterious events? Check yourself by reading the solutions.

**Solution 1:** It may seem cruel that predators like mountain lions eat deer. Most often, though, the predators catch old or sick prey. By removing these members of the herd, more of the limited amount of available food is left for the young, healthy animals. In the Kaibab Forest, the protected deer population grew larger, consuming nearly all of the leaves, twigs, and other vegetation that made up their food supply. When the food was gone, the deer starved until only the number that could live on the available food was left.

**Solution 2:** It's normal for bark beetles to attack pine and spruce trees. Normally, woodpeckers eat enough of these pests to keep them under control. After the storm, however, the woodpeckers were not able to reach the beetles, which were beneath the trees lying on the ground. The beetle population increased rapidly until it was greater than all the hungry woodpeckers could eat. The large number of beetles spread to healthy forest trees too, and within a few years, most of the trees in the forest were dead as a result of the booming beetle population.

# Biosphere II: Earth's Sequel

Biosphere II is a terrarium on a grand scale. It's a 2.5-acre, totally sealed environment, the largest completely separate environment in the world. It was named this because the earth has a biosphere, a life-supporting zone enveloping the planet. The biosphere is a fragile zone as thin compared with the earth as apple peel compared with an apple.

Biosphere II is closed off from the surrounding air by a double-paned glass dome and sealed off from the soil by a stainless-steel plate. There are seven environmental regions within this mini-world: a rain forest, a savannah, a salt-water marsh, a freshwater marsh, an ocean, a desert, and an agricultural area. Biosphere II will serve as the entire world for more than 3,000 types of plants and animals, plus eight people—four men and four women—for two years.

To make it possible for Biosphere II to

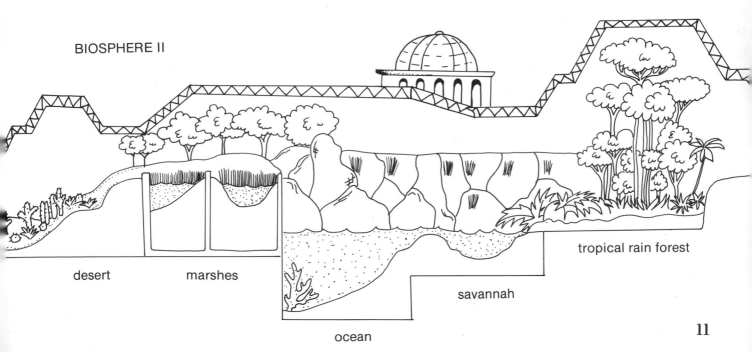

BIOSPHERE II

desert    marshes

ocean

savannah

tropical rain forest

11

be self-sustaining for such a long time, systems sometimes mimic nature and other times make use of technology. No one has ever created such a large, totally sealed glass cover before. Because Biosphere II is located in the hot desert region between Tucson and Phoenix, Arizona, the huge dome's double-paned glass not only seals out air and rain, but allows water to run between its two layers to help cool the interior environments.

Big fans help keep air flowing inside this miniworld, and computers control the temperature to create seasons. The desert, for example, will drop to as low as the upper thirties during the simulated winter and be very hot during the summer. The rain forest's temperature, though, stays constantly between sixty and ninety degrees Fahrenheit.

Overhead sprinklers, also computer controlled, respond to monitors in the soil to produce "rain" when the natural water cycle needs supplementation. Controlling growing conditions will make it possible for "Biosphereans"— the human residents of Biosphere II—to control the oxygen to carbon dioxide ratio. When there's too much carbon dioxide, desert and savannah plants can be encouraged to grow, and use up the supply.

Because the structure of the huge glass dome is very rigid, researchers had a special problem to solve. How would it be possible to keep differences between the air pressure outside the dome and that inside Biosphere II from making the dome explode or implode (collapse inward)? The solution was to add structures called "lungs." They work like a bellows, expanding when the pressure inside builds up and needs to be released and allowing air back inside when the pressure drops.

The animals and plants inhabiting Biosphere II were carefully selected to create food chains containing several different species at each level. That way if one of the species happened to die out, the chain wouldn't be broken. Many of the plants in the rain forest were selected because they can be used for food or even as medicine. Some animals, such as bats and hummingbirds, were chosen because they're pollinators. Many plants cannot reproduce unless animals spread the pollen from one flower to another. Biosphere II also includes an insectary, a building specifically devoted to raising helpful insects, such as the praying mantis and ladybug. Any time insect pests get out of control in an environment, these insects can be released as exterminators. Chemical pesticides would be too harmful to the environment in such a small world. A few animals, such as butterflies, were also included simply because they're beautiful.

To complete the nutrient cycle, wastes are recycled. Sewage is cleansed and used as fertilizer. Wastewater is filtered and used for watering plants. And drinking water is collected from the "rain" produced in the water cycle that goes on naturally inside Biosphere II just as it does inside your terrarium—and on the earth.

Biosphere II is providing an opportunity to develop and test some of the technology that will be needed to colonize the moon or even Mars. It also provides a way to study how the earth's ecosystems function.

# Why Do We Need Forests?

Take a deep breath. Did you enjoy that fresh supply of oxygen? More than likely you have a forest to thank for it. Through the process of photosynthesis, green plants soak up carbon dioxide, a gas given off by animals, as they convert sunlight into chemical energy in the form of sugars and starches. And during this process they release into the air the oxygen that which animals need to survive. In this way, green plants help maintain the balance of carbon dioxide and oxygen gases in the air. Grasses growing on a savannah, algae in the oceans, and even hardy plants inhabiting deserts and arctic tundra help. Forests, though, contain nearly three-fourths of all the world's plants, and so do the most to soak up excess carbon dioxide and add to the world's oxygen supply.

Check the map below to find where in the world the forests are located. Based on the climate and the main types of trees, forests are grouped into three categories—boreal, temperate, and tropical rain forests.

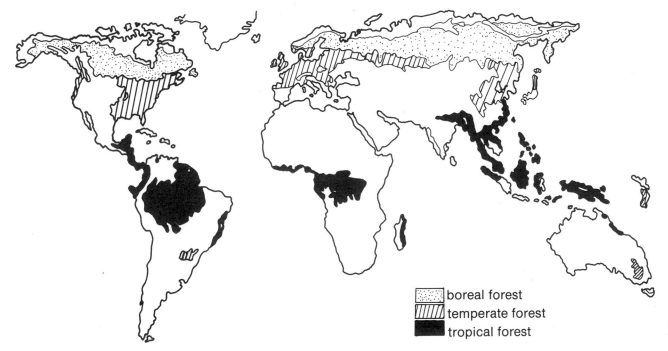

: boreal forest

||||: temperate forest

■ tropical forest

Boreal forests were named after Boreas, the Greek god of the north wind. It was a suitable choice because the trees and animals in such a forest face a very cold climate with a short growing season. Most of the trees in these forests are conifers, such as hemlocks, spruces, firs, and pines. Timber wolves, black bears, and moose stay year-round, but birds are mainly summer residents.

Temperate forests may have evergreen conifers in their northern extremes, but most of the trees are deciduous hardwoods, such as oaks, maples, and beeches. These trees shed their leaves once a year. White-tailed deer, porcupines, squirrels, and many birds are happily at home here.

Tropical rain forests are hot, humid places that receive more than sixty inches of rain a year, with some getting as much as 400 inches! Although these forests cover less than 10 percent of the earth's surface, they contain about half of the world's total growing wood and about two-fifths of the world's different types of plants and animals.

Besides providing animals with life-supporting oxygen, forests are also an important part of the food chain for many animals. Other forest products include maple syrup from maple trees; chicle, which is used to make chewing gum, from the sap of sapodilla trees; resins, which are used to produce turpentine, from longleaf and slash pines; and, of course, wood, which is used to build homes and produce paper and paper products.

Forests also help the land. Trees act as windbreaks that keep soil from blowing away. Tree roots hold water in the ground and help anchor the soil so heavy rains don't wash it away. Decaying leaves and even dead trees decompose and form humus, which help make the soil fertile.

Imagine what the earth would be like without any forests. How would your life change? What would you miss the most?

# What Would You Do?

Indiana only has one national forest, the Hoosier National Forest. Even though it represents less than 1 percent of the state, it's still the state's largest area of publicly owned land. What happens to this particular forest is up to all the state's taxpayers. Hoosier National Forest, like all national forests, is managed by the U.S. Forest Service.

As part of the forest's management plan, timbering—cutting trees for lumber and pulp—would be allowed in about half of the forest. Gas and oil could be drilled for on about half of the land, and mining would be permitted on thousands of acres. Conservationists want to reduce the timber harvest and protect old-growth areas. An old-growth forest contains very old, large trees that are home to wildlife that can survive only in such areas. Conservationists also want to totally prohibit oil, gas, and mining exploration. On the other hand, producing lumber, petroleum products, and mining resources means jobs and money for the entire state.

Whether to preserve Hoosier National Forest as a wilderness or use its natural resources is not an easy decision. Before deciding what you think should be done, visit the library and find out more about forests. If there is a national forest in your area, visit it. Ask questions about how that forest is being managed and what kinds of changes management policies have caused in the past ten years.

To share your opinion about what should be done to the Hoosier National Forest, write to Hoosier National Forest Supervisor, 811 Constitution Avenue, Bedford, Indiana 47421. If the idea of caring for forests appeals to you, you might consider a career in the forest service. For more information write for a copy of *Careers: Professional and Administrative Careers in the Forest Service* from the U.S. Department of Agriculture Forest Service, South Agricultural Building, Independence Avenue, Washington, D.C. 20250.

# Adopt a Tree

Choose a tree near your home to really study. Pick one whose branches you can easily reach and examine. And follow the steps listed below, which were suggested by a horticulturist—a tree doctor—for checking up on your tree's health.

First find out what kind of tree it is. Its leaves, twigs with buds, and its bark are all clues that can help when you look in books that identify different types of trees.

Next, see how much root room your tree has. The greatest threat to a tree's general good health is having its root area restricted.

Roots are covered with tiny, hairlike strands called root hairs that penetrate the spaces between soil particles, absorbing oxygen, water, and needed minerals. Even very large trees rarely have a root system that goes deep into the ground. Most of the roots spread out just ten to twelve inches below the surface. This root system stretches from four to seven times farther than the outer edge of the tree's leafy canopy. Look up, find the end of the longest branch over your head, and measure along the ground from the tree trunk to that point. Multiply that distance by four and plot this total distance from the trunk in each of the four main compass headings—north, south, east, and west. Is anything covering the roots? The roots will die under areas where the soil is hard-packed or topped with concrete or asphalt. If a large area of the tree's root system is damaged, the tree is in trouble.

Finally, check out these indicators of your tree's health:

1. Are the leaves normal size? Check in a book about trees or use the leaf shape to find several other trees of the same type and compare leaf size.

2. Do any of the leaves look yellowish when they should be green?

3. Do you see any new growth from the past year? To find out, you'll need to look at five twigs. Find the bud at the end of the twig. Then measure from that bud to the first set of encircling rings—the location of last year's terminal bud. Add together the measurements for all five twigs and divide by five to compute the average twig growth.

4. Look for any obvious wounds on the trunk, such as holes or tunnels through the bark. Also look for webs among the branches, galls (bumps) on twigs, and dripping sap—all signs of an insect attack.

Because trees are green plants, they need healthy green leaves to carry on photosynthesis and make the food the tree needs to live and grow. Healthy-looking leaves and twig growth are signs that the tree is doing well. If there is evidence of insect pests, or if the tree simply doesn't look healthy, report the problem to the owner of the property where the tree is located or ask for help in contacting the department responsible for your local city trees. The problem could be caused by pollution. (See "Acid Rain Keeps Falling on My Head," page 43.) It might be the result of overwatering, the lack of an essential mineral, or disease.

← bud scale scars
(These show position of previous terminal bud.)

# INSECTS THAT ATTACK TREES

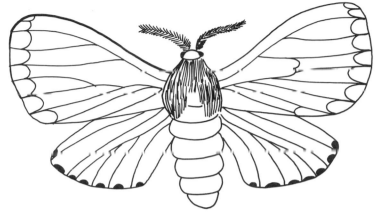

adult tent caterpillar

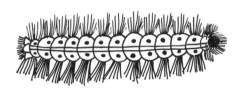

tent caterpillar larva

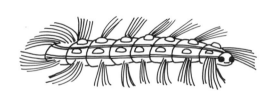

gypsy moth larva

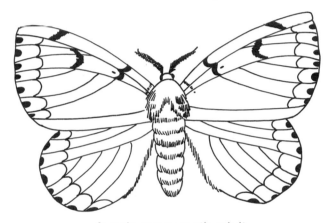

female gypsy moth adult

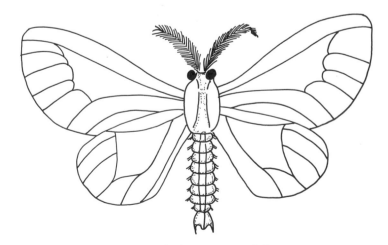

male bagworm adult

bagworm larvae in bag

Trees get sick too. In the early 1900s, a fungus disease called the chestnut blight entered North America (scientists think it came in on ornamental trees imported from Asia). Within a few years, most of the beautiful American chestnut trees that had once thrived from Maine along the Appalachian Mountains to Alabama were dead. So a tree with problems can't always be helped. Most of the time, however, it's possible to restore the tree to a healthy life.

In the United States, the American Forestry Association has launched an effort called Global ReLeaf, with the goal of having people plant 100 million new trees in cities and towns by 1992. For more information on this program, write to Global ReLeaf, P.O. Box 2000, Washington, D.C. 20013, or call 1-900-420-4545. (The cost of the call is a $5.00 tax-deductible donation to this project, so ask an adult's permission before calling.)

# Trees Are Air Conditioners

To some extent, trees help clean pollutants from the air. Look closely at leaves, particularly on roadside trees. A white or grayish coating is evidence that the trees have trapped some of the dust that would otherwise be polluting the air. Leaves with a waxy surface trap even more than leaves without this coating. Trees may absorb sulfur dioxide and other chemical pollutants, helping to purify the air. By acting as a windbreak, trees also slow down the air causing it to drop its load of polluting particles.

Try these activities on a warm, sunny day to discover two other ways trees condition the air.

1. Hold any indoor/outdoor thermometer waist high to check the temperature as you stand in full sun.

Next, move into a tree's shade. Wait about five minutes to allow time for the thermometer to adjust. Then check the temperature again, holding the thermometer about waist high so all the conditions are the same—except for the shade. The results are definitely cooler in the shade.

2. Slip a plastic bag over the leafy end of a branch you can easily reach. Pick one that is not exposed to full sunlight, or wait for a partly cloudy day. Slip an identical bag over a bare branch. Tie the open end of both bags tightly shut. After three hours, check the bags before removing them from the branches. Surprise—the bag on the leafy branch will be foggy and the

inner surface will be coated with little droplets of water while the other one will be nearly dry. Moisture was released by the tree through its leaves. On a warm, sunny day many gallons of water may enter the air from a single large tree. Think how much moisture a whole forest can produce!

# Rain Forests Are Special

Tropical rain forests are found in only 7 percent of the world, but they play a vital part in sustaining life on all the earth. One reason they're so important is that these forests have a tremendous effect on the amount of carbon dioxide in the atmosphere. Not only do the living trees act like "lungs," absorbing carbon dioxide gas and generating oxygen, they also store carbon. Burning trees, which has been the traditional method for clearing the land for farming and cattle grazing, releases great quantities of carbon, which combine with oxygen in the air to form carbon dioxide. Rotting vegetation also adds carbon dioxide to the air. Scientists fear that too much carbon dioxide in the air can change the world's climate. (See "Longer Summers Could Cause Hot Problems," page 36.)

Tropical rain forests are also the world's best zoos—natural habitats with a year-round breeding season for about half of all the known kinds of plants and animals in the world. These species are valued not only because they exist, but because they are each links in food chains. As you've already discovered, a missing link can cause many other species to suffer, and possibly be destroyed.

Rain forest plants also are the source of many medicines. For example, a chemical called vincristine, which is extracted from the rosy periwinkle that grows in Madagascar's tropical rain forest, has successfully been used to treat childhood leukemia. Quinine, which for many years was the only successful medicine for the

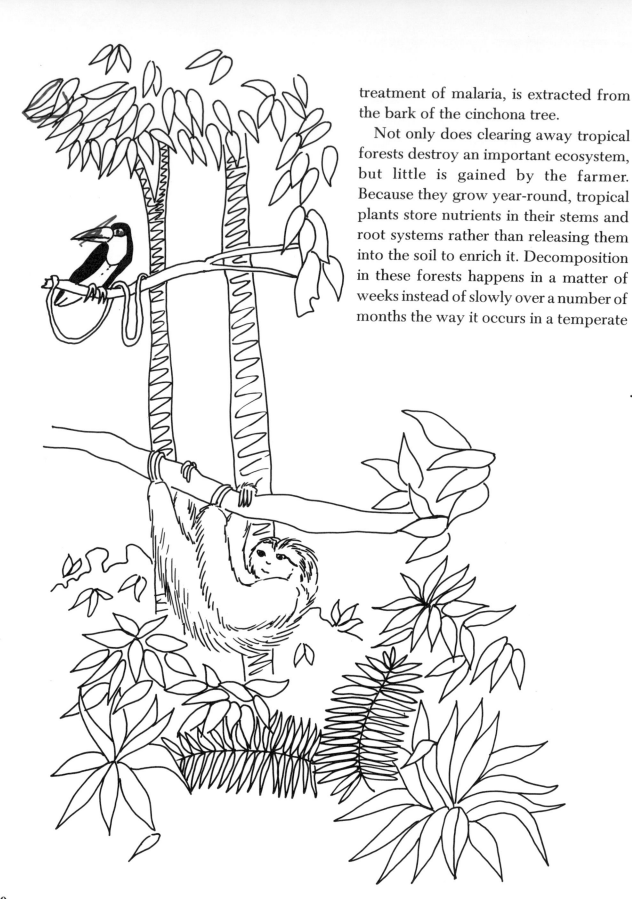

treatment of malaria, is extracted from the bark of the cinchona tree.

Not only does clearing away tropical forests destroy an important ecosystem, but little is gained by the farmer. Because they grow year-round, tropical plants store nutrients in their stems and root systems rather than releasing them into the soil to enrich it. Decomposition in these forests happens in a matter of weeks instead of slowly over a number of months the way it occurs in a temperate forest. The released minerals are quickly used by fast-growing plants. This results in a soil with very limited fertility. Within two or three years, the cleared forest land is no longer productive, and the farmers move on. The deserted land contains too few nutrients to become reforested, and, at best, sprouts a scrubby cover of plants. More often, the ground remains bare.

The Amazon Basin is the biggest remaining tropical rain forest, covering a little over a billion acres and stretching over parts of Brazil, Peru, Venezuela, and Bolivia. Part of the problem of protecting this region is that it is under the control of several different governments with very different views on how its natural resources should be used.

# After the Forest Is Gone

To see what happens to the impoverished soil left behind when rain-forest land is farmed and then abandoned, try this experiment. Outdoors, line a large box with plastic garbage bags, or work in a child's plastic swimming pool. Build a dirt island, at least six inches high in the middle of your container. You may need to mix in a little water to make the soil pack together, but be careful not to create mud. Give your island mountains and valleys if you like. Carefully pour water around your island to create a mini-ocean. Use a sprinkling can to "rain" on your model island. Let it rain hard for several minutes, simulating the heavy tropical rainfall. Then study the results. You'll see that the water carved gullies in the land. Where did the soil go? Check the mini-ocean.

The island of Haiti was called "the jewel of the Caribbean" by early ex-

plorers because of all that its lush rain-forest–covered lands had to offer. Today, with its forests gone, much of this island is unproductive, and its inhabitants—plants, animals, and people—are struggling to survive.

# Fast Fact

What can you do in one minute? Scientists estimate that about 100 acres of the remaining tropical rain forest environment is being cleared or at least seriously disturbed every minute. One acre is about the size of a football field, minus the end zones. So to get an idea of how much rain-forest land is damaged every minute, try to picture 100 football fields. Of course, by the time you've finished imagining that, several more minutes will have passed. The loss in trees and homes for animals keeps on adding up.

# Study Wildlife at the Zoo

You don't have to travel to Madagascar to observe the behavior of lemurs, to Zaire to study okapis, to Brazil to watch capybaras, or to the tropical forests of Borneo and Sumatra to learn more about orangutans. You can track down and observe these animals at a zoo.

Of course you'll want to make one visit to the zoo just to see all the animals that reside there. Then choose two or three animals to focus on during your next visit. If your local zoo has special ecosystem displays, such as a rain forest or an African veld with a number of different animals residing together the way they would in nature, select at least one of these animals too.

Next, prepare to be a zoologist (someone who studies animals) by reading books about the animals you'll be studying. Find out where in the world they normally live, what they eat, how they raise their young, if they are solitary or social, and if they are most active at night or during the day. Then when you go to the zoo again, plan to spend three 20 minute periods at different times of day observing the animal.

During an observation session, sit very quietly—just as a zoologist would in the wild—listening and watching. Take along a notebook to write down what you see and hear. If possible, talk to a curator to find out how big the animal is (height, length, and weight), its age and sex, what it likes to eat, and how much and how often it eats. Try to discover the answers to these questions as you observe.

1. What features make the animal especially suited for surviving in its natural habitat?
2. Is the local temperature similar to or very different from that in its natural habitat? How does the animal respond to the temperature?
3. If more than one animal is present, how do the animals interact?
4. How does the animal groom itself?
5. In what way, if any, does the animal communicate?
6. If you have the opportunity to watch the animal eat, how does it tackle its food?
7. Is the animal's behavior different during one time of day than another? If so, in what way?

If you enjoy this experience, you may want to think about a career as a zoologist.

# A Brief History of Trash

People have always had trash. One of the ways scientists have learned about how cavemen lived is by studying their trash dumps. For centuries, in fact, people simply hauled the trash to a convenient location near their home, piled it up, and left it up to nature to dispose of it. Your grandparents probably remember trips to the city dump.

Then, as the number of people grew and the cities expanded, there was less room for dumping and the amount of material being thrown away was increasing. It's estimated that every man, woman, and child in the United States throws away a little over a ton of trash each year. In many developing countries, dumps are still the only method for disposing of trash and garbage even though they are unsightly, smelly places likely to encourage rats and flies, which spread disease. In the city of Manila, in the Philippine Islands, approximately 20,000 people actually live on a mountain of trash, sifting through the refuse to find bits of food and reusable items.

In most cities, however, the local dump doesn't become a suburb. In fact, cities have attempted to get rid of their refuse in a number of ways. They've tried burning it at the dump site, but found that it produced stinky smoke that covered the city in a dirty-brown cloud. They have also dumped wastes into lakes, rivers, and the ocean, until people realized that the trash and chemicals were killing the wildlife living in these water ecosystems. Polluting the water with toxic (poisonous) materials also greatly increased the cost of producing clean drinking water. The solution, for a time, seemed to be to bury the trash and garbage in landfills.

A landfill begins as a trench or natural depression. Each day, as the wastes are dumped, bulldozers pack them together and cover the pile with a six- to eight-inch cover of dirt. When the pile reaches a height of thirty feet, it's capped off with a five-foot thick coating of clay and another pile is started beside it. This cap discourages rats and insects. However, since the bottom and sides are exposed to the soil, oil and toxic chemicals can seep through; they may even flow into nearby lakes or wells, which provide water for the community.

To protect their water resources, communities began to choose landfill sites far away from water sources. This made it even harder to find places to dump the steadily increasing stream of waste materials. Some cities in the United States

Freshkills, the largest landfill in the world, according to the Guinness Book of World Records, is located on Staten Island, New York. Over 15,000 tons of trash are dumped there daily, covering 2,400 acres and heaped up to form three pyramid-shaped mountains. The largest of these will be 505 feet high when completed. While it was once believed that this landfill would be filled by the turn of the century, recycling has extended this deadline indefinitely. Eventually, when it's capped over, Freshkills will be used as parkland.

and Europe that have used up all available landfill sites are now shipping their trash to other places. Undeveloped countries are becoming more cautious, though, about accepting trash that may contain toxic chemicals. For example, in 1987 a garbage barge loaded with refuse from Islip, New York, was refused dumping privileges in North Carolina because it carried potentially hazardous wastes. During a nearly three-month search for a place to unload, Florida, Alabama, Mississippi, Louisiana, Mexico, the Bahamas, and Belize all refused to accept Islip's trash. Finally, the waste was returned to New York and incinerated.

Unlike the early method of just igniting piles of trash at dump sites, the incineration process is designed to prevent escaping pollutants. Special smokestack "scrubbers" clean the air before it is released. And the heat from burning the garbage is used to produce steam, which can be used directly to heat buildings or to generate electricity. Although the ash that is leftover after the trash is burned must still be trucked to a landfill for disposal, this only represents about 10 to 20 percent of the original amount of waste.

Landfills are being made more carefully now too. The trench or depression is lined with plastic and clay to stop leaks—similar to the way you put a plastic bag in a trash can.

# Digging into Landfills

Landfills are supposed to be a place where fungi (molds), bacteria, and other microbes have time to dine on garbage, such as food, paper, and yard clippings, decomposing it and returning nutrients, like nitrogen, to the soil. That's what microbes do to a dead plant or a dead animal lying on the forest floor. But how successful are these organisms at breaking down what gets dumped in landfills?

To find out what goes on in a landfill, follow these steps to build a model of one. You'll need a clear glass quart jar, potting soil, two banana slices, plastic wrap, two penny-sized pieces of cooked hot dog, a handful of grass clippings, a sheet of newspaper, a chunk of a Styrofoam cup, and a two-inch square of aluminum foil.

1. Fill the jar one-third full with soil. Place a slice of banana, a piece of hot dog, and a small piece of the newspaper in the jar.
2. Add enough soil to fill the jar about half full. Wrap the second slice of banana and hot dog together in

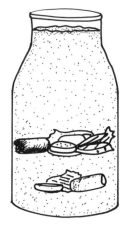

plastic. Next, wrap the grass clippings separately in plastic and place both packages on top of the soil in the jar. Add the Styrofoam chunk, the aluminum foil, and another piece of newspaper.

3. Finally, add soil until the jar is nearly full and pack it down. Place your model landfill in a warm, shaded place.

Readable newspapers have been unearthed after more than twenty years in a landfill. Even food items, such as hot dogs and lettuce, have been dug up only slightly changed after about five years. And it's estimated that aluminum cans, glass bottles, and plastic products of all types are likely to stay just as they are for centuries.

Wait three weeks and then spread out newspapers and dump the contents of the landfill onto it. You may discover some mold growing on the unwrapped banana and hot dog, but odds are everything else will be the same.

Studies made by digging into landfills have revealed that materials are more often entombed there than decomposed. Even things like food and paper, which would normally break down if exposed to the oxygen in the air and sunlight, don't change much when they're buried.

1952 newspaper

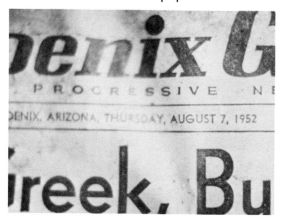

corn

carrots

# Make Natural Fertilizer from Garbage

Composting is a method people have used for many years to let microbes change garbage into humus or decayed plant and animal material. Not only does humus give soil the nutrients plants need to grow, it also helps loosen soil. This lets oxygen and water flow down through the soil and makes it easier for plant roots to spread out.

To make your own compost pile, the first thing you need is a big box—one that is at least three feet wide and three feet deep. Place the box outdoors well away from the house because a well-functioning compost pile usually smells. Line the bottom and sides with plastic garbage bags. Next, build up layers of the following materials about eight inches thick: twigs or wood chips, grass clippings or food scraps, and soil. Pour on enough water to moisten but not soak the pile. Then repeat the layers and watering until the box is two-thirds full.

Although the microorganisms in your compost are too small to be seen without special instruments, they're in there. In fact, a pinch of soil no bigger than a kidney bean may contain as many as 100 million bacteria, fungi, microscopic green algae, and tiny one-celled animals.

And it doesn't take long for this dirty bunch to go to work. As they eat, the complex materials in the wastes are gradually changed into simple substances. And during this process, nutrients—especially nitrogen and phosphorus, which plants need to be healthy and strong—are released.

It will take between one and two months for the composting process to completely transform the garbage and plant material into dark brown, crumbly humus. During this time, you'll need to use a shovel to mix the pile every three to four days. This will provide the microorganisms with the oxygen they need, help move the fully broken-down material out of the center area, and release the smelly gases that are likely to build up. When there is no longer any recognizable sign of the material you used to build the compost, the humus is ready to mix into the soil.

Composting is an especially effective way to save landfill space. Grass clippings and yard wastes account for as much as 20 percent of all solid wastes in landfills. In a number of European countries, cities are already separating and composting yard and food wastes.

Now the idea is catching on in the United States. Florida is one of ten states where it's already against the law to include leaves, twigs, or grass clippings with the trash. And Agripost, Inc. in Pompano Beach, Florida, is one of a number of companies that has made composting their business.

Unlike the mini–compost pile you built, Agripost starts with as much as 800 tons of waste per day and can produce about 175,000 tons of humus in a year's time. When the waste first arrives, it's spread out and any potentially dangerous items, such as old car batteries and propane tanks, are removed. Next, the waste is sent through a grinding process that transforms everything—even glass, plastic, and rubber—into particles about the

size of sand grains. Then this material goes to a six-acre indoor composting area. Even though this compost pile is many times larger than the one you built, what happens to the material during the composting process is identical. The finished material is bagged and sold to sod farms, golf courses, home gardeners, and even to cities to use in covering filled landfills.

# Can You Use Less More Often?

Stopping waste before it builds up is called *precycling*, and it's a great way to help keep the earth from becoming buried in trash. Check this list for things you can do.

• Don't collect more bags than you absolutely have to. When you buy things at several different stores at a mall, ask to put later purchases in the bag you already have. Even better, take a tote bag with you from home and don't accept any of the store's bags.

• Avoid buying things that have unnecessary packaging. For example, slice your own cheese instead of buying the kind that has each slice individually wrapped. Buy large sizes of dishwashing soap, detergents, cereals, and other items that store well. If you prefer to use things in smaller packages, transfer the product from the larger containers into small ones that you already have on hand.

• Prepare foods, such as hamburgers, at home rather than buying take-out.

If you buy fast food, ask for it in paper containers.

• Skip items that are designed to be used only a few times and then thrown away, such as disposable contact lenses. And buy items that can be reused, such as rechargeable batteries.

• Find uses for things that would otherwise become trash. For example, use the back of junk mail and greeting cards as notepads.

• Shop with care. Choose things that are made to last. And be sure that what you buy is something you really need or want.

# Does Your Home Have Hazardous Wastes?

Anything that can harm people or the environment is considered a hazard, and a surprising number of things found around the house fit into this category. Of course, even though your house is likely to have a number of these items, there probably isn't a lot of any one thing. These materials only become a problem when you throw them away or pour them down the drain. Then your hazardous wastes mix and combine with those dumped by your neighbors. As the quantities add up, so does the size of the problem.

Copy the checklist below and look for these items around your house. If you find any of them, call your local waste collection service, your local public health agency, or local environmental agency for places where these materials may be taken to be disposed of safely.

**In the kitchen or laundry room, look for:** drain cleaner, window cleaner, bleach, ammonia, oven cleaner, spot remover, disinfectant.

**In the garage:** paint thinners and strippers, spray cans, lacquers and varnishes, latex and oil-based paints, antifreeze, battery acid, gasoline, motor oil, weed killers, ant and rodent killers.

**Elsewhere:** hobby supplies, such as artist's paints, glues for model building, photographic chemicals.

# Just as Good the Second Time Around

While the earth's resources are in limited supply, they don't have to be "used up." Perhaps as much as 50 percent of what's thrown away could be reused or recycled. The key is to sort trash based on the basic material it's made of, such as paper, glass, aluminum or other metals, plastic, rubber, and food and yard wastes. This is necessary because, while a few items, like soda bottles, are simply cleaned and refilled, most are used as a source for basic materials. Junk cars, for example, are cut up and sorted into different kinds of metal: copper, steel, chrome, and aluminum. These materials may then be used to produce a new car or they may provide materials for pipes or part of a park bench. Whenever there is even the remote danger of contamination, recycled materials are not used for food containers.

Recycling not only saves the resource material, it also saves energy. Recycling generally requires less energy than producing a product from new raw materials. Aluminum is a good example. It takes over 90 percent less energy to recycle this metal than it does to produce aluminum from ore or rocks containing the metal. Reusing glass also results in savings. Crushing the old glass into tiny bits called cullet and melting these to make new glass requires between 40 and 60 percent less energy than melting sand to make glass. Again, sorting counts because to be successfully recycled, glass must be separated by color—clear, amber, or green. Besides producing new containers, recycled glass is used to manufacture fiberglass and to pave roads. Watch for black asphalt roads that sparkle in the sun. Glass bits are mixed with asphalt to create a strong, long-lasting road surface.

recycling symbol

# What's in the Trash?

Make a copy of the chart below. Then keep track of what you throw away for one day by putting a check on the chart next to the type of item each time you throw it away. If you throw away writing paper three times, for example, that column would get three check marks.

Don't really throw your trash away during the day, though. Save it in your own personal trash bag. And at the end of the day, weigh what you've collected.

**Personal Trash Chart**

**Writing paper**

**Magazines**

**Paper packaging**

**Wood items (Popsicle sticks)**

**Food**

**Glass containers**

**Soft plastic (soft drink bottles or clear wrap)**

**Hard plastic (plastic spoons)**

**Polystyrene (Styrofoam cups)**

**Aluminum (soft drink cans or foil)**

**Any other kind of metal (tin cans)**

**Anything else**

Now take the trash challenge. Save and keep track of your trash for another day, but this time make an effort to throw away as little as possible. Challenge your friends to join in the fun and see who can throw away the least. The earth will be the real winner.

# Be a Recycling Inventor

Of course it took some pretty creative thinking to design egg cartons, create plastic rings to hold clusters of cans together, and develop a plastic container that would hold a carbonated soft drink without blowing up like a balloon. Now it's your turn to do some creative brainstorming. Try to think of at least six different ways you could reuse containers once they're empty. Look around the house for containers that could move on to a new career. Here are a few to get you started.

**Play Jug Toss.** Play with a soft foam ball. The object of the game is to use the jug scoops to toss the ball from one person to another. The player doing the tossing calls the name of the player who must catch the ball. Any player who fails to catch the ball collects one letter of the word "Oops." When all four letters are collected by the same person, he or she must drop out of the game. The winner is the person remaining when everyone else has spelled "O-O-P-S."

**Grow a Kitchen Herb Garden.** Fresh herbs give foods terrific flavor. So start a mini-herb garden. Use a sharp pencil to make several small holes in the bottom of three polystyrene cups. Fill the cups with potting soil. Cut the top off a two-liter plastic soft drink bottle, and set the cups inside the remaining container. Buy herb seeds, such as basil or parsley, at a plant nursery and follow the planting directions on the package. Set the container in a warm, well-lit spot that isn't exposed to full sunlight. Cover with clear plastic wrap—recycled, of course—until the plants sprout.

By the way, the cut-off top of the bottle can be used as a funnel or a pipe for blowing big bubbles.

**Add Color to Your Light.** Save your balloons when they pop. Stretch the colored rubber over the bulb end of your flashlight, pull it smooth, and anchor it in place with a rubber band. Then go into a dark room or closet and switch on the flashlight for a special effect. Try making the beams of several different flashlights different colors and explore what happens when spots of these colored lights overlap.

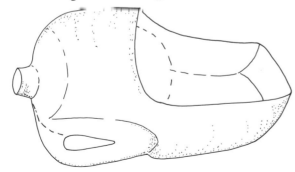

# Paper Facts

Here's some news about paper that may amaze you.

• Although it takes about twenty years for a loblolly (southern) pine to grow to be twenty feet tall, this large tree can be cut down with a chain saw in just fifteen minutes.

• Only specially designed facilities can recycle paper. This is because the paper to be recycled must first be sorted to remove any materials that aren't paper, such as clay used to make the glossy pages of newspapers and magazines. Next the old paper must be mixed with water and beaten to separate the fibers, and chemicals are added to remove the printing ink. After being thoroughly washed, the pulp is finally pressed, dried, and rolled into sheets of new paper.

• Even recycled paper is partially made with new wood pulp. Every time paper is recycled, the wood fibers become shorter and weaker. Adding some new wood pulp helps keep the newsprint strong and durable.

• Recycling paper costs more than making paper from new wood pulp, but it saves trees. It takes about 75,000 trees to produce enough paper for the press run of just one Sunday edition of the *New York Times*. Returning a three-and-a-half-foot tall stack of newspapers will save one twenty-foot-tall tree.

• Besides newspapers, it's important to recycle computer printout paper and cardboard boxes. Since paper loses some strength when it's recycled, high quality office paper is especially good for recycling. It can be turned into lower quality paper, such as newsprint and grocery bags, the second time around.

• Paper makes up 40 percent of all solid waste so recycling saves dumping costs and space. Recycling paper also saves energy. It takes 64 percent less energy to manufacture recycled paper than to produce paper entirely from fresh wood pulp.

• Unfortunately, because recycled paper does take special facilities, it's more expensive. So only a small percentage of the paper purchased by the world's market is recycled paper. The United States could change this since it is the leading consumer of newsprint, using 40 percent of the world's supply.

# What about Plastics?

Products made of plastics are every where. In fact, take a few minutes out to go on a plastics hunt. See how many different things you can find that are at least partially made of plastics. Don't miss these items: plastic tableware, toothbrush, eyeglass frames, foam pillow, helmet, plastic pipes, plastic parts on a kitchen appliance, plastic parts on a car, plastic film (check a video tape or cassette tape), plastic parts on luggage, plastic raincoat, packing peanuts, plastic containers in the kitchen or laundry room, and plastic parts on any of your clothes—especially anything you have on right now. Plastics are often used in place of wood, glass, rubber, and metal because they're less expensive to produce, weigh less, and may even be more durable. They can also be safer to use. If dropped, a plastic bottle won't shatter, for example. The biggest complaint against plastics used to be that they couldn't be recycled. Today, however, many plastics are recyclable.

Just as there are different kinds of metals, there are many different kinds of plastic, each with its own special attributes. All plastics, though, have one thing in common. The molecules, or tiny chemical building blocks, of these materials form long chains. The special features of a particular type of plastic—whether it's rigid or flexible, for example—depends on the chemicals that make up these chains, the shape of the chains, and even how groups of chains are arranged.

There are three main kinds of plastics: PET (polyethylene terephthalate), used for soft drink bottles and other containers; HDPE (high density polyethylene), used for milk and juice jugs; and polystyrene foam, used for coffee cups, egg cartons, and other foam products. Collect a soft drink bottle, a milk jug, and a foam coffee cup and compare these three kinds of plastics. How are they alike? How are they different? You can always tell PET plastic from other kinds because it's clear, not cloudy. And polystyrenes always have a foamy appearance.

During the recycling process, the different types of plastics are sorted. Then the material being recycled is broken down into small pieces and combined with new plastic material to produce fresh products. Because it isn't possible to be sure the recycled material is free of all contaminants, recycled plastic is never used for food containers, but rather for many other products, such as flowerpots, toys, and fiberfill for jackets and pillows. Plastic *lumber* can even be made from polystyrene foam. Plastic trash collected in a number of our national parks is being recycled and returned to the parks in the form of benches, signs, and walkways over wet areas, among other things.

Of course the only way for plastic—just like paper, aluminum, or glass—to be recycled is for you to take part in the process. You must sort the plastic items from the rest of your trash and deliver them to a recycling center. You may be lucky enough to live in a community that has curbside pickup for recycling. If not, check the *Yellow Pages* of your telephone book under recycling. Or contact your local or state level department of environmental resources. You could even help organize a local clean-up and recycling program. The Glad Company will supply how-to information, bags, hats, and cash to participating groups if your community joins in their national Bag-a-thon, scheduled annually from the second week of March until the second week of June. Call 1-800-262-GLAD to find out more about this program.

# Longer Summers Could Cause Hot Problems

Many scientists think the earth's overall climate is slowly warming. In fact, the 1980s produced the four hottest years thus far this century, and 1988 was the warmest since 1860. Experts estimate that even warmer weather is yet to come—as much as seven degrees warmer on the average during the first fifty years of the twenty-first century. Milder winters and longer summers sound good at first, but a warming trend means some major changes for the earth.

For one thing, the sea level is likely to rise as polar regions warm and the ice at the north and south poles begins to melt. This may put half of Florida, much of the Netherlands, and many other low-lying areas underwater. Whole cities would have to be abandoned and people would need to find space to live farther inland.

Agricultural crops would also be significantly affected by global warming. Besides flooding farmland, changes in precipitation patterns could result in some areas being much drier than they now are and other regions being much wetter. We've already experienced several major droughts during the 1980s that seriously damaged grain production in the midwestern farm regions of the United States and the steppes of the Soviet Union. Of course, this warming trend wouldn't be all bad. Historically cold regions, such as parts of Canada, for example, would have a longer growing season, making it possible to grow crops, such as corn and soybeans, that don't normally do well in the far north.

So what's causing global warming? To find out try this. Collect two identical shoe boxes. Remove the lids, cover the bottom of the boxes with black construction paper, and place an indoor/outdoor thermometer inside each box. Set the boxes side by side in a window where they are exposed to full sunlight. Wait five minutes to allow the thermometers time to adjust, then check and write down the temperature on each thermometer. Next, cover the top of one box with clear plastic wrap. Pull it tight and use tape to hold it in place and seal the edges. Wait fifteen minutes this time. Uncover the box, and immediately read the temperature on the thermometers in both boxes.

The air in the box with the clear plastic wrap cover will have increased in temperature more than that in the uncovered box. Scientists commonly call what happened the *greenhouse effect*, since, like a greenhouse, the air trapped inside is warmer than the air surrounding it.

The sun is the heat source for the earth, but the atmosphere, the air surrounding the earth, is warmed only slightly by sunlight passing through it. Instead, objects on the earth's surface absorb the light energy and change it to heat energy. As the rocks and soil and even buildings

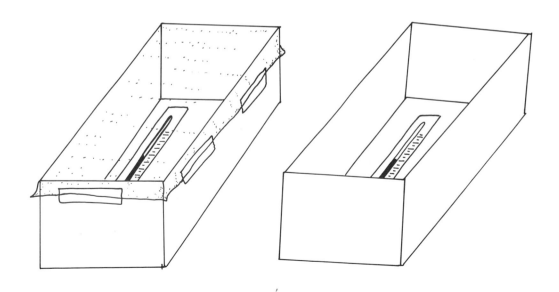

GREENHOUSE EFFECT

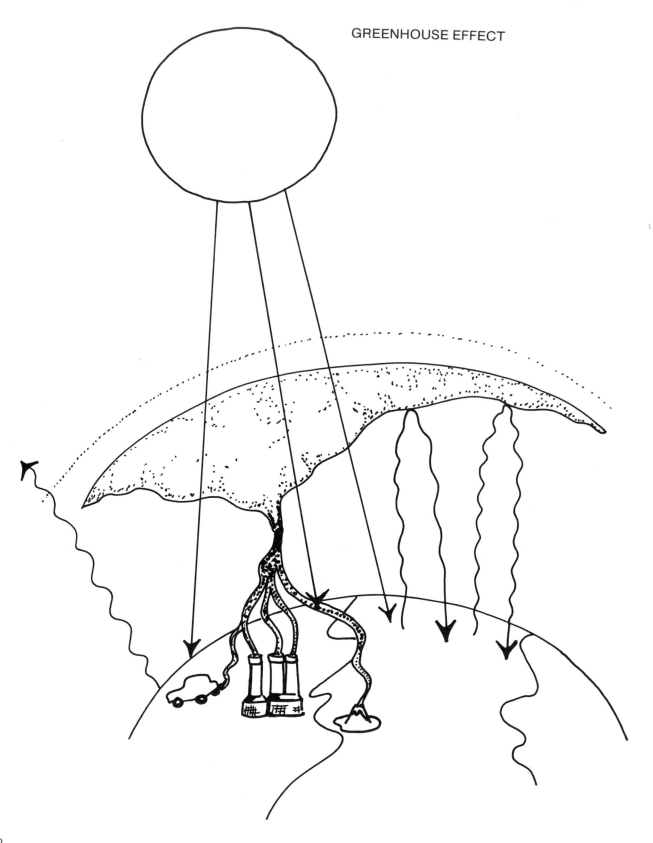

warm up, they radiate heat into the air, warming it. Much of this radiated heat energy would normally rise and eventually be lost in space. But some is absorbed by carbon dioxide and other heat-trapping gases in the air and bounced back to the earth's surface. This acts like the clear wrap cover on the box, trapping the heat and making the temperature climb.

As you'll remember, it's perfectly normal for there to be some carbon dioxide gas in the atmosphere. This is the gas animals breathe out and green plants need to complete the photosynthesis process and produce food. However, the burning of fossil fuels—coal, gas, and oil—to generate energy for industry, and especially to run cars and trucks, releases carbon that was "locked up" in these fuels. When the carbon combines with oxygen in the air, it becomes carbon dioxide. The more fossil fuels that are burned, the more carbon dioxide builds up. And when the amount becomes more than green plants can consume, the amount of heat being absorbed and bounced back to the earth increases too.

The atmosphere's heat-trapping ability has been increased even more by the emission of other heat-trapping gases: methane, nitrogen oxide, and chlorofluorocarbons (CFCs). Methane gas is given off by decaying plant matter from swamps, rice paddies, and landfills. Nitrogen oxide, like carbon, also comes from burning fossil fuels, and from fertilizers. CFCs come from aerosol propellants and lost coolant from air conditioning and refrigeration units.

The trouble is that while the effect of these heat-trapping gases can be seen, the gases themselves are invisible. So it's impossible to see them escaping into the atmosphere. That doesn't mean these heat-trapping gases can't be controlled. In 1989 there was an international agreement to limit the use of CFCs with the goal of cutting use in half by 1999. This was an important step since an effort by one country alone would have little effect if the rest of the world continued to spew these gases into the atmosphere.

You can help by reading labels. Don't buy or use anything that contains the following chemicals: CFC-11, CFC-12, CFC-113, CFC-114, CFC-115, Halon-1201, Halon-1211, or Halon-2402. Also avoid using the car air conditioner since this type of refrigeration system still uses CFCs. Better yet, avoid using the family car. Walking and biking are great exercise, and leaving the car at home helps cut down on the production of carbon dioxide and nitrogen oxide. And don't forget to plant trees, if you can. Plant at home or share in your community's effort. Trees can reduce the amount of heat-absorbing gases in the air and their shade can help keep you cool in a warming world.

# How Much Excess CO₂ Do You Add?

Besides what you breathe out, you cause some carbon dioxide ($CO_2$) gas to be given off into the atmosphere every time you use electricity generated by a coal- or oil-fired power plant. Any time you use water heated by natural gas or cook something with natural gas, you're causing a little more $CO_2$ to be given off. You create the greatest amount of excess carbon dioxide, though, when you travel in a car. According to the Environmental Protection Agency, the exhaust of the average twenty-mile-per-gallon car equals one pound of carbon dioxide for every mile it moves.

So how much $CO_2$ does your family car add to the atmosphere in just one day? To find out, write down the mileage listing that appears on the car before it moves for the first time in the morning. (You may need to have an adult point this reading out to you.) Then copy down the mileage again when the car is parked for the last time at the end of the day. Subtract the number you listed in the morning from the afternoon's number to find out how many miles the car was driven during the day. This number is about the number of pounds of carbon dioxide gas your family's car spewed out (it may be a little less or more depending on the actual number of miles per gallon the car averages). Actually, the car also probably spewed out a little more than that amount if it had to sit in traffic or ran while waiting in a drive-through line. If your family has more than one car, keep track of the miles driven by each car and then add all of these together to figure out the total amount of excess carbon dioxide given off by your family cars in one day.

Now hold a family meeting and try to think of ways to help cut down this amount. Obviously, driving less would help the most. Could anyone carpool, take a bus, or walk instead of ride? Could the family vote to avoid using drive-through lines?

# More Sunscreen Needed

Heat buildup isn't the only change taking place as gases being spewed out on the earth drift up high into the atmosphere. Some of these gases have also helped cause a decrease in the amount of ozone in the upper atmosphere. Ozone is a molecule made up of three oxygen atoms. The presence of ozone is important in the atmosphere because it absorbs ultraviolet (UV) radiation streaming toward the earth from the sun. Exposure to UV radiation is what causes you to get a sunburn. And an increase in the amount of UV radiation reaching the earth's surface could damage plant tissues and cause more people to develop skin cancers. Normally, the ozone layer acts as a shield by screening out 99 percent of this harmful radiation. But an increase in the amount of pollutants reaching the upper atmosphere has disrupted the normal process that maintains an adequate suppy of ozone.

When ozone molecules absorb UV radiation, this reaction causes the ozone molecule ($O_3$) to split apart into an oxygen molecule ($O_2$) and an oxygen atom (O). Oxygen molecules may also absorb ultraviolet radiation and split into two separate oxygen atoms. Since free oxygen atoms readily hook up with other nearby oxygen atoms, new molecules of ozone are formed and the cycle begins again. Under normal conditions, the amount of ozone being broken down by absorbing UV radiation is balanced by the formation of new ozone molecules. Other reactive substances, though, such as CFCs escaping from cooling systems and aerosol containers, also react with ozone molecules causing them to break apart. When this happens, the supply of ozone to absorb UV radiation is dimin-

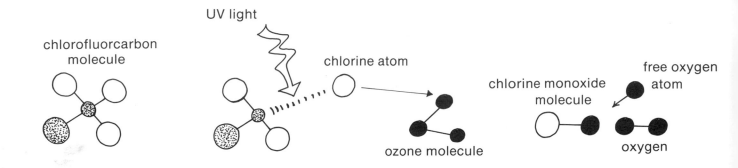

chlorofluorcarbon molecule

UV light

chlorine atom

ozone molecule

chlorine monoxide molecule

free oxygen atom

oxygen

Ironically, although ozone high in the atmosphere is very helpful, when too much ozone is close to the ground it's an ingredient in smog. Smog is the dirty brown haze that lurks over big cities like Dallas and Los Angeles and even affects our view of the Grand Canyon. Smog is harmful to plants and makes it harder for people to breathe.

ished and more of this harmful radiation reaches the earth's surface.

Although the ozone layer never completely disappears, it sometimes becomes so thin that scientists say there's a "hole" in it. Scientific measurements show that the thinning of the ozone layer is worse toward the poles because air flow patterns tend to carry chemical pollutants in that direction. Measurements also indicate that the thinning is usually worse in the spring.

Luckily, the damage to the ozone layer isn't permanent. All the things being done to protect the atmosphere and stop global warming will help heal the ozone layer too. Repair will take time, though—perhaps as much as several hundred years.

When a layer of warm air sits above cooler air, polluted city air cannot rise and escape. This condition, called an inversion layer, is responsible for engulfing Los Angeles in a brown smog cloud for much of the time from May to November each year.

warm air

cool air

# Acid Rain Keeps Falling on My Head

Acid rain is a term used to refer to any precipitation, including rain, snow, sleet, fog, and even dry pollutants, which fall from the sky and form acids when they encounter moisture. Acid precipitation is nothing new. Rain is always slightly acidic because carbon dioxide, which is always in the atmosphere, dissolves in water vapor to form a weak acid. Much stronger acids form, though, when industries, power plants, and cars and trucks burn fossil fuels and give off sulfur and nitrogen oxide. Rain as acid as lemon juice has been measured in Norway. Parts of Pennsylvania and West Virginia have recorded acid rain that was even stronger—as strong as vinegar. Unfortunately, the source of the chemicals that have produced the acid rain may be hundreds of miles away in another state or even another country. Tall smokestacks release the sulfur and nitrogen oxide high in the air where winds carry them away. So making laws that will stop such pollution becomes difficult and causes heated debates.

The effect of acid rain is obvious, though. It causes minerals to dissolve more rapidly than normal and when these seep into lakes, the ecosystem is greatly disturbed. For example, some lakes in eastern North America have had such a large increase in the amount of metals poisonous to fish that the lakes are considered dying or dead. Marble and metal buildings and sculptures are also "eaten away" by acid rain, and many trees are damaged. Large parts of the forests in West Germany have died as a result of acid rain, and forests—especially pine and spruce forests—from New England to southern Georgia show serious leaf damage. Canada, which has been especially affected, is angry because the main source of the acid rain falling in that country is believed to be the coal-fired power plants in the United States.

# Acid Rain in Your Miniworld

To observe the effects of acid rain on plants for yourself, give your miniworld some acid rain. Every other day for two weeks remove the cover, mist the plants very lightly with vinegar, and reseal. Look for changes in leaf color. Check for any signs of wilting. Watch for evidence of new growth. Write down everything you see in a notebook.

Finally, sprinkle some grass seed on any exposed areas of soil and seal. Continue to observe for three weeks after you stop adding "acid rain." Do the seeds sprout? How does the time needed for sprouting and the number of young sprouts you see compare to what you first observed when you started your miniworld?

# Check for Dirty Air

Besides the often invisible chemicals, air may also be contaminated by particulate matter, tiny bits of dirt. These windblown bits may be from forest fires, industrial processing, and even the result of burning solid wastes at a landfill. The simple test that follows will let you check how much particulates effect the quality of the air around you. You will need twelve flat coffee filters, a ruler, a pencil, a sheet of notebook paper, a yardstick, a permanent marker, petroleum jelly, strong tape (such as electrician's tape), and a magnifying glass.

First, copy the chart below and select four locations near your home for the test. Spread a thin coating of petroleum jelly over the outside of each of the coffee filters. (The tiny bits of particu-late matter will stick to this film). Select test sites, such as a telephone pole or a tree, to which the filters can be attached. Measure up three feet from the ground and tape or tack three filters one above the other at each site. Write the location you selected on the chart and predict whether you think the air is clean or polluted by particulate matter in this particular area.

Next, trace around a clean coffee filter on a sheet of notebook paper. Use the ruler to draw a square inside the entire center of this shape. Divide this square into equal one-inch squares. Go over these lines with the permanent marker so the grid will show through a coffee filter when you place it on top of the square. You may need to hold this up to a sunny

| Place | What you predict polluted/clean | Number of squares with dirt particles | What you conclude polluted/clean |
|---|---|---|---|
|  |  |  |  |
|  |  |  |  |
|  |  |  |  |
|  |  |  |  |

window to see through the filter more easily.

After twenty-four hours collect the coffee filters at one location. Hold the filters, one at a time, over the grid you made and look at the surface with the magnifying glass. Count the number of squares in which you see dirt particles. Total the number of squares for all three filters at one location and divide that total by three to find the average number of squares showing particulate matter. Record the average on the chart. Repeat this check of each filter at the other locations you chose. Finally, analyze the results you collected and draw a conclusion about whether the air in each location is polluted or clean.

# Making Air Healthier

Protecting the air is the law in the United States thanks to the Clean Air Act of 1963 and later amendments that make it even stronger. The diagrams below show some air-cleaning devices that help industries clean up the air they exhaust so we can all breathe easier.

Many big U.S. cities have reduced smokestack pollution by as much as 90 percent. Installing special devices called catalytic converters in automobiles has also helped to clean up the air. Because soot, dust, and chemicals are carried by winds, air pollution is still a major problem globally. China and Eastern European countries like Poland and Czechoslovakia pour tons of soot and sulfur dioxide into the air from coal-burning factories and home heaters. In the Americas, Mexico City's famously poor air is soiled by industry and by the city's millions of cars and buses, then trapped by tall surrounding mountains.

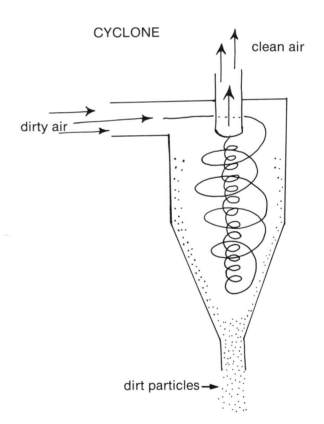

CYCLONE

clean air

dirty air

dirt particles →

The swirling air causes big particles of dirt to hit the sides, fall out, and drop out through the bottom.

BAGHOUSE

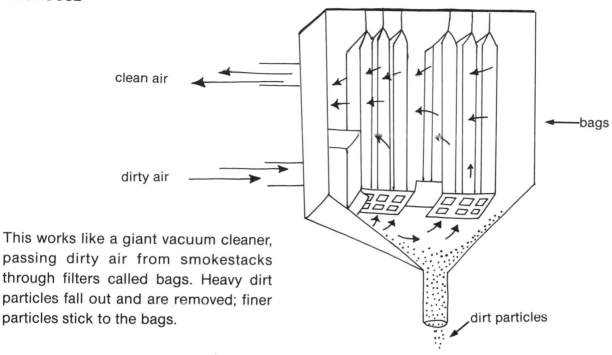

clean air

dirty air

bags

dirt particles

This works like a giant vacuum cleaner, passing dirty air from smokestacks through filters called bags. Heavy dirt particles fall out and are removed; finer particles stick to the bags.

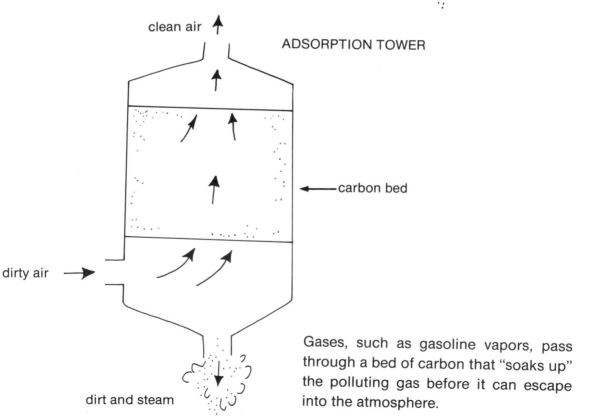

clean air

ADSORPTION TOWER

carbon bed

dirty air

dirt and steam

Gases, such as gasoline vapors, pass through a bed of carbon that "soaks up" the polluting gas before it can escape into the atmosphere.

## ELECTROSTATIC PRECIPITATOR

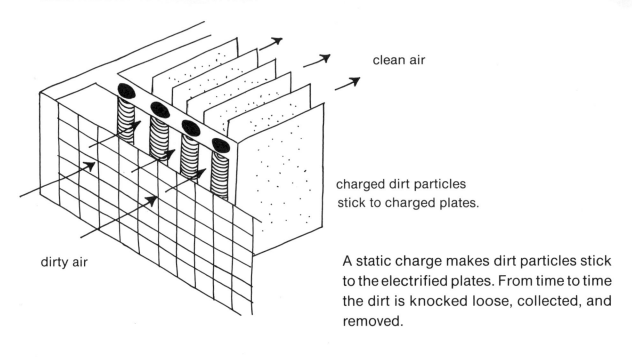

clean air

charged dirt particles
stick to charged plates.

dirty air

A static charge makes dirt particles stick
to the electrified plates. From time to time
the dirt is knocked loose, collected, and
removed.

## SCRUBBER

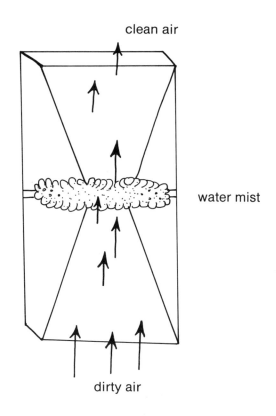

clean air

water mist

dirty air

As dirty air passes through a water mist,
dust particles are filtered out. The water
mist is often injected with limestone
powder to help extract the dirt particles.

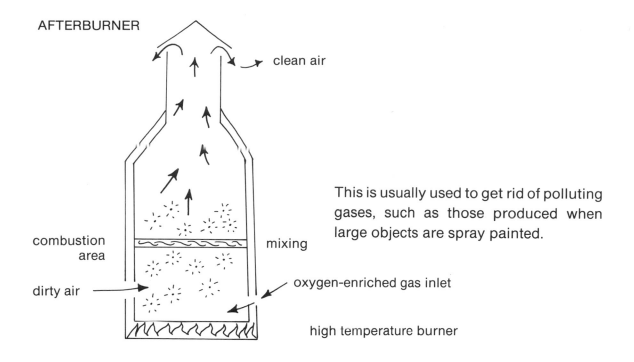

AFTERBURNER

clean air

This is usually used to get rid of polluting gases, such as those produced when large objects are spray painted.

combustion area

mixing

dirty air

oxygen-enriched gas inlet

high temperature burner

# Rivers in Danger

The dumping of trash and chemicals isn't the only problem threatening rivers. Anything that alters a river's natural rate of flow or its purity effects the river's ecosystem, and endangers the animals and plants that live in the water and along the shore.

For example, plans are underway to divert a sixteen-mile stretch of the Klamath River, in Oregon, for a hydro-electric power plant. The Klamath, which flows from Oregon into California, is the home of trout and many predator birds. It's also a beautiful river

and popular for white-water rafting. Changing its flow pattern would seriously effect all of these.

Fortunately, people are hard at work trying to correct problems that have put rivers at risk. The effort made by the Nashua River Watershed Association, in Massachusetts, is one of many success stories.

Wastes from a half dozen paper mills, plus city sewage, had left more than a fifty-mile stretch of the Nashua River able to support only bacteria and sewage worms. When it was possible to see the surface of the river through the floating waste, the water was red, blue, green, or mustard yellow, depending on the color of dye being dumped by the mills. And signs were posted to warn people approaching river crossings to close their car windows to avoid the smell. The Nashua River was commonly called the "Nausea River" because, besides looking bad, it smelled awful.

Today, thanks to combined local, state, and national efforts to set regulations and build water treatment plants, the river is healthy and beautiful. It's once again home to otter, bass, and other wildlife. The water is clean enough to see the river bottom, which is sandy instead of covered with sewage. The Nashua River now attracts fishermen, and in a few years, should be clean enough for swimming.

# Adopt a Stream or River

Do you have a river or stream in your community? Adopt it. Then follow the *Check It Out* guide below to monitor conditions on this waterway and check for ways you can help protect it.

## Check It Out

1. Check the temperature of the water. Tie a pool or aquarium thermometer to a line and toss it into the stream. Be sure the line is long enough for you to remain safe, far from the water's edge. Wait several minutes to allow time for the temperature to adjust before retrieving the thermometer and reading the temperature. Fish do best when the water in a river or stream is around seventy degrees Fahrenheit. If the temperature is greater, the fish can't reproduce. And if the water is too warm, they die.

2. Observe whether you can see the bottom clearly near the shore or whether the water is cloudy. Look for signs of soil erosion that could be clouding the water. Also check for trash in the water and observe whether or not the water smells unpleasant.

3. Notice how much of the water's surface is exposed to direct sunlight.

Write down the date and record your initial observations in a journal. Then check and update your observations at least once a month. Besides any immediate problems you observe, any changes you discover over time may mean trouble. Make an effort to know your stream's or river's background. Find out where it's coming from—whether it flows through cities, past industries, or along farm fields. Try to learn if the stream or river is used for drinking water, recreation, fishing, or waste disposal. Talk to a local conservationist or a biologist about what kinds of aquatic life lives in the stream or river. Also try to discover any efforts that have been made to control flooding.

Because healthy streams and rivers are beautiful, be sure also to spend some time just enjoying your adopted waterway. Hike along it or sit quietly and observe. What do you see? What do you hear? What do you appreciate most about this steam or river?

June is American Rivers Month in the United States. Write to American Rivers, 801 Pennsylvania Avenue, S.W., Suite 303, Washington, D.C. 20003, for more information on how to protect your stream or river all year long and how to organize a clean-up along its shores in June.

# Water: Good to the Last Drop

Another way to help protect streams, rivers, and lakes is by conserving water. Although water covers three-fourths of the earth, 97 percent of that water is salty. Of the remaining 3 percent that is fresh water, about three-fourths is frozen in glaciers and the polar ice caps. That only leaves a tiny fraction available for drinking, cooking, washing, watering crops, and for the numerous industrial processes that require water, such as manufacturing paper and steel. Even though water, unlike fossil fuels, is a renewable resource, overuse is placing a strain on the supply of pure fresh water.

If nature is allowed to take its course, rainwater that soaks into the ground builds up. Gradually this groundwater seeps into lakes, rivers, and streams, filling them. If the groundwater is drawn away and used, though, the new supplies can't keep up with the demand.

The solution, of course, is to use less fresh water. But to decide in which ways you can cut back, you first need to find out how much water you use in a day. Start by copying the chart on page 52. Then keep track of your consumption by listing each time you use water and checking the *Water Use* guide to see the average amount the particular use consumed. At the end of the day, add up the total number of gallons you used.

Even though the following aren't on your list, don't forget that you're also using water each time you use something

| Water use | Average gallon(s) per use |
|---|---|
|  |  |
|  |  |

**Water Use**

| | |
|---|---:|
| Getting a drink of water | ¼ gallon |
| Toilet flush | 5 gallons |
| Shower (approximately 2–3 minutes with water on full force) | 20 gallons |
| Tub bath (full tub) | 30 gallons |
| Brushing teeth | ¼ gallon |
| Washing only hands or face | 2 gallons |
| Cooking a meal* | 3 gallons |
| Washing clothes in washing machine* | |
|    Small load | 22 gallons |
|    Average load | 30 gallons |
|    Large load | 49 gallons |
| Washing dishes for one meal by hand* | 8 gallons |
| Running automatic dishwasher* | |
|    Standard cycle | 12 gallons |
|    Potscrubber cycle | 15 gallons |

*Divide this amount by the number of people in your family to determine your share of the water consumed.

that required water as part of its production process. For example, it takes as much as seventy-five gallons of water to produce a single ear of corn, six gallons of water is needed for every gallon of gasoline produced, and sixty-five gallons is needed to manufacture enough steel to make a bicycle.

You may want to total your water use for several different days and compute the average amount you used (add the totals and divide by the number of days you kept track). Then think of ways that you can cut down on the amount without cutting down on what you really need. For example, does it make a difference how hard the water is running while you wash your hands or brush your teeth? To find out, close the drain in the kitchen sink. Next, turn the water on full force and let it run for fifteen seconds. Be ready to shut the water off fast when the time is up. Then bail the water into an empty gallon milk jug to measure it, dumping the water into a bucket each time the jug is full, and write down the total you collected. Save all the test water to pour on some thirsty plants.

Repeat, turning the water on medium force, and again with the faucet on just enough to produce a thin stream.

As you will discover, the force of the flow *does* make a big difference, so try suggesting to your family that they replace showerheads and faucets with low-flow models. These can reduce the amount of water usage by as much as 50 percent. Also, placing a half-gallon plastic bottle filled with water in the toilet tank will reduce the amount of water used during each flush. (The toilet is designed to fill based on the water level in the tank. Don't use a brick to raise the water level, though. It's likely to crumble and clog lines.) You can also help reduce your family's water usage by encouraging your parents to repair leaky faucets and to wash their cars only when absolutely necessary. When the lawn needs watering, suggest doing it in the morning or evening when water evaporation or loss to the air is slowest.

# Cleaning Water to Be Used Again

It's not enough for there to be an adequate supply of fresh water. You want the water you drink and use to taste good, smell good, and look good. It must also be safe, meaning that the water must be free of any harmful chemicals or disease-causing organisms. Since fresh water is in such limited supply, it's lucky that water is recyclable.

This activity will let you explore how wastewater from your toilets, tubs, dishwasher, and clothes washer, plus rainwater draining into storm sewers, can be cleaned and reused. First you need to make some dirty water. Fill a quart jar half full of tap water. Then drop in a few pebbles, a small handful of grass clippings, two tablespoonsful of soil, and a couple of drops of red food coloring. Stir to mix well.

To clean your polluted water the way a city waste treatment plant does, you'll need a second container, (such as a metal mixing bowl) a piece of wire screen, an eggbeater, a coffee filter, chlorine bleach (laundry bleach), and an eye-dropper. Now follow these steps to clean the water.

1. When the dirty water first enters the treatment plant, it's screened to remove any large particles. Place the wire screen over the second container and pour the water through the screen. Get rid of whatever was trapped and clean the empty jar.

2. Next the water is pumped into a settling tank where dirt and gravel sink to the bottom. Let the water you poured into the second container set for several hours or until the soil has

settled, forming a layer on the bottom.

3. In some systems, the water is next mixed with air and pollution-eating bacteria. Pour the water into the clean jar, being careful not to mix in any of the settled debris. Clean out the container you just emptied, then pour the water back into it. Whip the water with the eggbeater to mix it with air and let it sit for several hours.

4. In a real plant, the water is allowed another opportunity to settle and may be filtered again by being pumped through beds of sand and gravel. Place the coffee filter over the mouth of the clean jar and pour the water into the jar through the filter. Be careful not to dump out any waste that has settled to the bottom.

5. Finally chlorine gas is pumped through the water to kill disease-causing organisms. Add chlorine bleach one drop at a time to the water you're treating until any trace of the red coloring is gone and the water appears clear.

Of course, the water you treated isn't really safe enough to drink, but now you know how water is recycled in water-treatment plants. If possible, arrange to visit your community's wastewater treatment plant to see it at work.

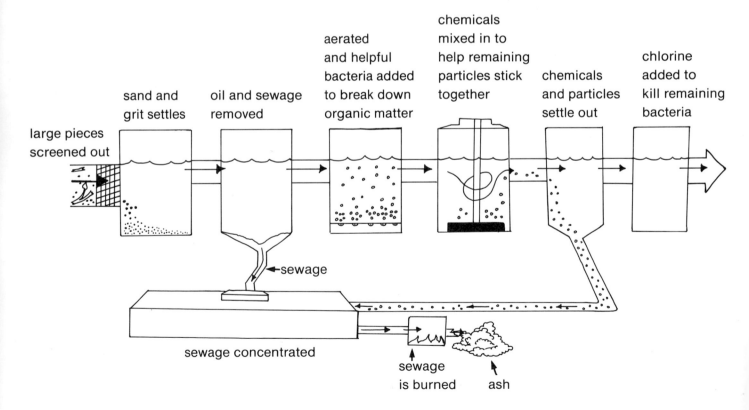

# Oil and Water Don't Mix

Since three-fourths of the earth is covered by oceans, it's not surprising that ocean ecosystems play a key role in the successful functioning of this planet's life-support systems. Green ocean plants—many of them tiny—that float on the surface help keep the amount of carbon dioxide and oxygen balanced in the atmosphere. And ocean food chains are a vital source of food for the earth's human population. Unfortunately, it has taken major oil spills, such as when the Exxon tanker *Valdez* spilled eleven million gallons of oil in Alaska's Prince William Sound, and when more than 462 million gallons were dumped into the Persian Gulf during the war with Iraq to demonstrate that the ocean isn't as capable of dealing with pollution as was once believed.

Oil companies argue that spilled oil doesn't cause long-term damage because it's biodegradable, meaning microorganisms use it as a food source. And when these microorganisms in the ocean break down the oil, the effect is the same as when decomposers break down decaying plant and animal material in the soil. The microorganisms help release nutrients that other plants can use to grow, so, oil companies claim, oil actually enriches the ocean to some extent. That might be true if the amount of oil was no greater than what the available microorganisms could handle and the oil was supplied slowly enough for them to have time to break it down. Oil spills, though, overwhelm the decomposing microorganisms and even destroy them. Dissolved chemicals in the oil can inhibit the growth of phytoplankton, the tiny green plants that are the basis of ocean food chains, for weeks or even months. And bigger animals and plants, such as fish, shellfish, and seaweed, become coated in oil and die.

To see what makes oil an even greater problem, fill a glass half full of water, add several drops of blue food coloring to make the water easier to see, and pour in several tablespoonsful of vegetable oil. Like an ocean spill, you can see that this oil floats on the surface. Most ocean life is concentrated at the surface and extends only as deep as sunlight penetrates. So spilled oil is especially damaging to ocean life. Even worse, the greatest concentrations of marine plants and animals are close to the coasts, which is where tanker traffic is heaviest and most offshore drilling operations are located.

When spilled oil reaches shore, the destruction extends to often fragile shore and marsh ecosystems. At sea, wave action and exposure to the weather causes the lighter parts of the oil to evaporate and the heavier parts to form tar balls, which sink. On shore, the effect and damage lasts longer. Eight years after a spill damaged the Wild River estuary, in New England, oil still pooled in footprints of anyone walking across the sand; shellfishing wasn't allowed because the animals were contaminated; and some animals, like fiddler crabs, still couldn't survive there.

# No Slick Solution

The demand for petroleum has been increasing by about 10 percent a year for the past fifty years. When armed conflict caused the shorter shipping route through the Suez Canal to be closed in the late 1950s, the shipping companies built bigger tankers. The biggest of these, the giant supertankers, are about a quarter of a mile long. With only the tank bulkheads (upright partitions separating parts of the ship) and an exterior metal shell for strength, these huge ships sag in the middle when waves lift the bow and stern, and bow up in the middle when this section is lifted by a wave. And they ride so low in the water that during storms massive waves smash across their decks. Exposed to so much physical stress, powered by only one motor, and lacking any backup navigational equipment, it's no wonder the tankers have problems and spills. While it's the big spills that attract worldwide attention, there are many more small spills every year—about 2,000 with an average loss of 100,000 gallons or less per spill, and as many as 7,000 or more with a loss of about 100 gallons. All the little spills add up, however.

Attempts have been made in the past and continue to be made to find sources of energy other than oil—ones that would ultimately be less expensive to obtain and more earth-friendly to use. Coal, wood, nuclear energy, solar energy, wind, geothermal energy from the earth's natural heat, water energy, tidal energy, and energy generated by decomposing garbage have all been tried. Each has resulted in some degree of success and presented its own set of disadvantages and problems. None of these alternate energy sources has proved as successful or as inexpensive as petroleum. As the supply of oil—a nonrenewable energy supply—dwindles, though, alternative sources will become a necessity.

# The Journey Continues

Now you know the basics about how your Spaceship Earth operates and what must be done to keep its life-support systems functioning. You've discovered the wonder and joy of a healthy environment, and you've investigated the problems that exist: pollution, a limited supply of available resources and space, and ecosystems that are being stressed by the needs and demands of a rapidly increasing human population. You are part of the first generation to fully understand that earth's biosphere—the thin zone of air, land, and water at the surface occupied by organisms—is limited in its ability to support life but can do the job if properly managed.

When you were younger, you were just a passenger on earth. But you've grown, gaining access to the environment. Besides new and enriching experiences, this increased access to the earth brings with it increased responsibility. At a bare minimum, it's important for you to recognize that whatever you can do to help repair and maintain the earth's life-support systems is in your best interest. How much you do to actually improve the earth is up to you.

There are parts of the earth that need safeguarding. And there are parts that need restoration. In every effort, it will be increasingly important for you to think globally and consider *all* of the earth, rather than just one city, state, or even one country. The challenges are great. The possibilities are intriguing. How much you accomplish is limited only by your imagination. The future is yours.

*This is definitely not the end.*
*This is the beginning.*

# Index

Acid precipitation, 43–44
Activities
   adopting a river, 50–51
   adopting a tree, 15–16
   being a recycling inventor, 33
   building a terrarium and using
      it for experiments, 1–3, 5
   checking for hazardous
      wastes, 30
   checking for dirty air, 45–46
   checking how trees affect
      the environment, 18–19
   composting, 27–29
   doing something about
      Hoosier National
      Forest, 14–15
   going on a plastics hunt, 35
   investigating causes of global
      warming, 37
   investigating ecosystems, 6–7
   investigating the effect of
      rainfall on bare land, 21
   investigating water use, 51–52
   making a model oil spill, 55
   observing how force of water
      affects flow, 52–53
   observing what happens in a
      model landfill, 25–26
   recycling water, 4–5
   solving ecosystem mysteries,
      10–11
   studying animals at the zoo,
      22–23
   studying personal trash, 32
   treating polluted water, 53–54
Adsorption tower, 47
Afterburner, 49
Agripost, Inc., 28–29
Aluminum. See Recycling
American Rivers, 51

Baghouse, 47
Biosphere II, 11–13
Boreal forests, 13–1

Carbon, 39
Carbon dioxide, 6–7, 12–13, 19,
   39–40, 43–44, 55
Catalytic converter, 46
Chlorofluorocarbons (CFCs),
   39, 43
Clean Air Act of 1963, 46

Composting, 27–29
Cyclone, 46
Decomposition, 9–10, 14, 25–26,
   27–29, 55
Dirty air
   general information, 45–46
   methods of cleaning, 46–49
   testing local air, 45–46
Ecospheres, 6
Ecosystem, 6–7, 8–10, 20, 23, 44,
   49, 55–56
Electrostatic precipitator, 48
Evaporation, 4
Folsome, Dr. Clair, 6
Food chain, 8–9, 14, 12, 19, 55
Forests
   careers in the forest service,
      15
   Hoosier National Forest,
      14–15
   of the world, 13–14, 19–21
Freshkills, 24
Garbage. See Trash
Glad Company. See Recycling
Glass. See Recycling
Global ReLeaf program, 18
Global warming, 36–39
Greenhouse effect, 37–39
Hazardous wastes. See Trash
Haiti, 21
Hoosier National Forest, 14–15
Humus, 27–29
Islip, New York, 25
Kaibab Forest, 10
Klamath River, 49–50
Landfills. See Trash
Manilla, 23
Methane gas, 39
Micrococcus, 9
Nashua River Watershed
   Association, 49–50
Nitrogen oxide, 39, 43–44
Nutrient cycle, 2, 9–10
Oil spill, 55–56
Oxygen, 2, 6–7, 12–15, 19, 27
Ozone, 41–43, 55
Paper. See Recycling
Photosynthesis, 6, 13, 16

Plastic. See Recycling
Precycling, 29–30
Prince William Sound. See Valdez
Pyramid of life, 8
Recycling
   aluminum, 25–26, 31–32
   finding new uses for trash, 33
   general information, 31
   Glad Company Bag-a-thon
      recycling program, 36
   glass, 31–32
   paper, 30–32, 34
   personal trash survey, 32
   plastic, 25–26, 28, 31–33,
      35–36
Scrubber, 25, 48
Smog, 42–43
Sulfur 4, 44
Sulfur dioxide, 46
Supertankers, 56
Temperate forests, 13–14, 20–21
Terrarium, 1–3, 5
Trash
   disposal in landfill, 24–27, 29
   garbage barge refused
      dumping privileges, 25
   hazardous waste, 30
   history of, 23–25
   incineration, 25
   recycling, 31–36
   world's largest landfill, 24
Tree
   as air conditioner, 18
   chestnut blight, 18
   global ReLeaf, 18
   insects that attack, 17
   structure, 15–16
Tropical rain forests, 13–14, 19–22
Ultraviolet (UV) radiation, 41–43
Valdez, 55
Water
   conservation, 51–53
   cycle, 4–5, 12
   polluted by oil, 55–56
   treatment, 53–54
   use, 52
White River National Forest,
   10–11
Wild River estuary, 56
Zoologist, 22–23